D0978880

The Magic School Bus® CHAPTER BOOK

The Magic School Bus®
CHAPTER BOOK

COLOR DAY RELAY

SCHOLASTIC INC.
New York   Toronto   London   Auckland   Sydney
Mexico City   New Delhi   Hong Kong   Buenos Aires

Written by Gail Herman.

Illustrations by Hope Gangloff.

Based on *The Magic School Bus* books
written by Joanna Cole and illustrated by Bruce Degen.

The author and editor would like to thank Dr. Eric Brewe of Hawaii Pacific University
for his expert advice in preparing this manuscript.

ISBN 0-439-56051-9

12 11 10 9 8 7 6 5 4 3   4/0   5/0   6/0   7/0   8/0   9/0

Designed by Louise Bova

Printed in the U.S.A.   40

First printing, May 2004

The Magic School Bus®
CHAPTER BOOK
A science

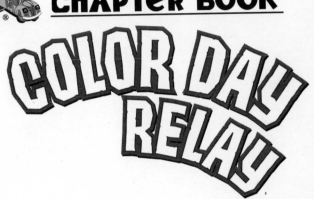

COLOR DAY RELAY

INTRODUCTION

Hi, my name is Ralphie. I'm one of the kids in Ms. Frizzle's class.

Maybe you've heard of Ms. Frizzle (sometimes we just call her the Friz). She is a terrific teacher, but a little strange. One of her favorite subjects is science, and she knows everything about it.

The Friz takes us on lots of field trips in the Magic School Bus. Believe me, it's not called *magic* for nothing! We never know what will happen once we step on board that bus.

Ms. Frizzle likes to surprise us, but we can usually tell when she is planning a special lesson. How? We just look at what she's wearing! So when the Friz announced that our class would be having Color Day, we expected her to show up in a colorful outfit. But we never expected the rainbow of surprises she had up her sleeve!

Just wait until you hear about our Color Day adventures. It wasn't just fun . . . it was brilliant!

CHAPTER 1

"Hurry, Ralphie, hurry," I muttered to myself. "Go, go, go!" I raced up the school steps, out of breath.

It was past 8:30. Any minute the school bell would ring. Any minute I would be late. Again.

B-r-r-ring!

"Oh, no!" I sighed. There was nothing I could do now. I was late, absolutely, positively late, for the second time this week.

I really had wanted to be on time today. It was Color Day! I wasn't sure what that meant, but it sounded like fun. And now I might miss it.

I pulled open the heavy door and

stepped inside the school lobby. I should have woken up earlier. I should have jumped out of bed as soon as Mom called me.

But no. I pulled the covers over my head and went back to sleep for ten minutes. Then I ate cereal, toast, and a banana, and got dressed. I was all ready to head out when my mom offered me some blueberry pancakes. So I had a little more breakfast.

Then I remembered something else, too. My new red baseball cap! I wanted to wear it today. I finally found it at the bottom of a pile of bats, balls, and gloves.

"Good-bye, Mom!" I called.

I plopped the hat on my head, grabbed my backpack, and ran outside.

Immediately, I ran back in. Lunch! I forgot to bring lunch! In fact, I had to pack it, too!

Now . . . at last . . . in the school lobby, I stopped to catch my breath. The halls were empty. I was probably the last kid to get to school. Again.

I walked as quickly as I could to my classroom.

The room was dark.

I was so late, everyone must have left. Ms. Frizzle had taken the class on some great field trip, leaving me behind.

Suddenly, the light flipped on. A window shade snapped open. I blinked. Everyone was still here! Liz, the class lizard, stood on a chair by the light switch. Ms. Frizzle was adjusting the window shades.

"Oh, Ralphie!" The Friz sounded happy to see me. "I'm glad you saw my little demonstration for Color Day."

"Color Day?" I repeated, confused. I hadn't expected Color Day to involve sitting around in the dark.

"At my old school, we had relay races and contests on Color Day," Phoebe said. "We never played with the lights."

The Friz laughed. "Well, Phoebe, you need color to have Color Day. And in order to see color, you need to have light."

I sat in my seat and thought this over. I felt excited about Color Day. But the light part of it? I didn't understand the connection.

Other kids felt the same way. Wanda raised her hand. "What do you mean, Ms. Frizzle? That if a light isn't shining on something, it doesn't have any color?"

Dorothy Ann — we call her D.A. — poked her head out from behind a pile of books. "That seems right to me!" she said. "When Liz turned off the lights, everything in the room looked dim and dark. Everything lost its color."

From the Desk of Ms. Frizzle

Light transfers energy in the forms of brightness and heat. Natural sources of light include the sun, other stars, and fire.

I had never thought much about color before. Something was a certain color — like my red baseball cap — and that was that. But I realized D.A. was right. Even if you see shapes in the dark, you can't tell what colors they are until you turn on a light.

But the whole thing was a little confusing. I twisted my baseball cap in my hands. "So my cap isn't really red until light hits it? It needs light to be red?"

"Absolutely light, I mean right, Ralphie!" Ms. Frizzle said. "Our eyes don't see it as red when there isn't any light. Don't worry if that seems confusing now — we'll explore it further during Color Day."

Keesha gazed at the sunlight streaming through the window. Then she looked up at the ceiling light. "Are you saying that light has color in it? It doesn't look colorful to me — it looks white. Or colorless."

"Correct," said the Friz. "Light rays all look the same. Some would say white. Some would say colorless. But sunlight is really made up of all colors. Red, blue, green, and the rest."

Sunlight, Sun Bright
by Keesha

Light traveling in a straight line — from the sun, a flashlight, or another source — is called a ray.

"So how does this color thing actually work?" asked Arnold. "But please don't turn off any more lights."

Ms. Frizzle stepped over to me. She flipped my cap onto her own head. "When light hits Ralphie's cap," she explained, "the baseball cap absorbs almost all the colors in white light."

Bright White Light

by Tim

What color is sunlight? To our eyes, it appears colorless. But every ray of sunlight contains all the colors in the visible spectrum – red, orange, yellow, green, blue, indigo, and violet. These colors combine to make what scientists call white light.

"Absorbs?" Wanda repeated. "Like a sponge absorbs water?"

"Yes. It soaks the light right up," Ms. Frizzle went on. "Except for red. The cap *reflects* the red light. Red light bounces off the cap, so the baseball cap looks red." Ms. Frizzle put the cap back on my head. Now I couldn't see it at all, and I couldn't see what she was getting at, either.

"Ms. Frizzle," I began.

Knock, knock.

I didn't get any further. Someone was knocking. Tim opened the classroom door. But no one was there.

Knock, knock.

"It's coming from outside!" said D.A.

At first I didn't see anything. Suddenly, a bright light flashed. Then I saw a man. He was sitting on a branch in the big oak tree near the window.

"Well, hello!" said Ms. Frizzle in a delighted voice. She opened the window. "Class, this is my friend Dr. Roy G. Biv."

Dr. Biv stepped from the branch, right into our classroom.

Dr. Biv? I thought. This guy didn't look much like a doctor, or a scientist for that matter. He wore a referee uniform — a crazy one. Instead of the usual black-and-white stripes, his stripes were all different colors. Red, orange, yellow, green . . . and he was wearing sunglasses. Inside!

"Why didn't he come through the door," I whispered to Keesha, "like any ordinary friend of Ms. Frizzle's?"

"Ralphie," Keesha whispered back, "you know Ms. Frizzle doesn't have any ordinary friends!"

"Dr. Biv is an expert on light," the Friz explained.

Okay, I thought. So that explains why he came in through the sunny window instead of the dark hallway. But still, he appeared kind of suddenly. And really, in that outfit he didn't look much like an expert on anything.

"Dr. Biv has agreed to help out with Color Day," Ms. Frizzle continued. "He'll run all the challenges and events. And he'll be the ref."

Just then Dr. Biv blew a referee whistle. Surprised at the noise, I jumped. Dr. Biv looked at me and raised his eyebrows.

Great. I had already made a lousy impression on the ref!

"We were just talking about white light," the Friz told Dr. Biv, "and how it's made up of all the colors."

Dr. Biv nodded. He reached into his pocket and pulled out some kind of object. "Does anybody know what this is?" he asked.

"It looks like a glass pyramid," Keesha volunteered.

"This is not an ordinary pyramid," Dr. Biv said. His voice boomed and echoed around the room. "It's called a prism."

D.A. looked up from her book. "What does it do?" she asked.

All the Light Moves
by Carlos

Isaac Newton was the first scientist to discover the connection between color and light. In 1664, he passed a beam of sunlight through a prism, then noted how the light spread into different colored rays. He passed these light rays through another prism, and they turned back into white light. His discovery? Color comes from light.

"Watch." Dr. Biv held the prism up to the window. Sunlight streamed into the prism on one side, and all the colors of the rainbow streamed out the other side. A whole band of colors that looked like a rainbow! "Red, orange, yellow, green, blue, indigo, violet," Dr. Biv declared.

Phoebe sighed. "That's so pretty."

"But how does the prism separate white light into all those colors?" I asked.

"The prism bends the light — each color at a different angle — so we get to see them all," the Friz explained.

I shook my head, confused. "In a way, I understand. But in a way, I don't."

Ms. Frizzle said, "Don't worry, Ralphie. We'll learn more about prisms and colors as we go through our Color Day activities. Everything will be crystal clear by the end of the morning."

Dr. Biv blew his whistle even louder. "Let the games begin!" he cried.

Games! I stood up, excited. "Color Day, here we come!"

CHAPTER 2

We all filed out the classroom door into the hallway. I was first in line. Me, Ralphie, "Late Is My Middle Name," first! What a great start for Color Day.

I figured we'd be going to the school field, so I turned right. But Ms. Frizzle led everyone the other way.

"Aren't we going outside?" I hurried after the class, last again. I was even behind Dorothy Ann, who was carting around a bunch of books.

"Expect the unexpected, Ralphie," Ms. Frizzle said. She ushered us into the gym.

We all stood around, not knowing what was next.

The Friz looked us over. "Now we'll divide the class into teams. Hmmm. Perhaps Dr. Biv could do the honors."

"Of course!" Now Dr. Biv looked us over. He polished his glasses so they gleamed. Then he stared at each and every one of us — hard. Arnold squirmed, turning red.

"You!" Dr. Biv said, pointing at him. "You're on the red team." He paused. "Along with . . ." He noted D.A.'s books, all with red covers. "Her. And . . ." His gaze stopped at me. "You, with the red baseball cap."

My heart sank. Me, D.A., and Arnold a team. Color Day is all about racing and being fast. Arnold is afraid to do anything quickly. D.A. is loaded down by books. And me? Well, I'm always late or last for everything. The red team didn't stand a chance.

Tim and Phoebe — with Liz, of course — were on the green team. Wanda, Keesha, and Carlos were on the blue team because they all wore blue jeans.

"Ready for the first race?" Ms. Frizzle asked.

"Ready!" the blue and green teams shouted. D.A., Arnold, and I just looked at one another.

"I call this first race White Lightning," Dr. Biv said. "You will need to move lightning quick."

Ms. Frizzle pointed out baskets filled with flashlights lined up along the gym wall. "Each team has a basket of flashlights to use to make white light. The first team to shine white light on this big sheet near Dr. Biv wins."

"All we have to do is race to our basket and turn on a flashlight?" I whispered to D.A. "Easy!"

"Ready . . ." said Dr. Biv. We crouched into starting position, ready to take off. "Set . . ." Everyone crouched lower. "Go!"

Ms. Frizzle dimmed the ceiling lights.

We raced toward the baskets. "Over here!" I shouted to D.A. and Arnold. I pulled out a flashlight. I switched it on. Oh, no! It had a red lightbulb, not a white one.

D.A. pulled out another flashlight. Green light. Arnold pulled out a third. Red again.

What should we do?

All around us, teams were having the same problem. They were shining yellow lights, purple lights, blue lights.

"Hey, where are the regular ones?" Keesha called out.

"If you mean white-light flashlights, there may be some in the baskets," Dr. Biv said. "Or maybe not."

"You'll have to search," the Friz explained, "or think about our classroom discussion."

D.A. snapped her fingers. "That's it!" she whispered. "If we get all the colors we saw in the prism and shine them at one spot, that will make white light!"

We sorted through the baskets. In no time, we had red, orange, yellow, green, blue, a really dark shade of blue that D.A. called indigo, and a light purple.

"I think that's it," said D.A.

I sneaked a peek at the other teams. They were going through their baskets, flicking on flashlights, turning off flashlights. Liz had even jumped inside a basket! They were all still searching for regular flashlights, I guessed. If we hurried, we could win!

"I'll bunch these lights together and shine them on the sheet," I said.

"Wait! There's too many for you to hold." Arnold reached to take a flashlight. "We'll do it together."

But I was in too much of a hurry to wait. I charged toward the sheet. Uh-oh, I dropped a flashlight. I bent to pick it up and dropped two more. D.A. and Arnold scurried over to help.

"Got it!" Tim cried. I looked up. He was shining a white-light flashlight against the sheet. He'd found one!

"Green team wins!" said Dr. Biv.

"But we were so close!" Arnold wailed.

"Yes." The Friz nodded. She scooped up all my dropped flashlights. Then she wound a big rubber band around them and flashed their lights against the sheet. White light!

Then Dr. Biv walked over carrying just

three flashlights — a red one, a green one, and a blue one. When he shone them at the sheet, their colors combined to make white light, too!

My mouth dropped open in surprise, but the Friz was nodding as if she had expected red, green, and blue light to make white.

Primary Colors of Light
by Ralphie

The primary colors of light are red, green, and blue. That means these colors can be used to make all other colors. The three primary colors together make white.

P.S. to D.A. and Arnold: I'm sorry I tried to hold all those flashlights at the same time. If I had known about the primary colors, I could have just used those three.

"You were close, red team," Ms. Frizzle told us. "Good thinking."

"Any points for good thinking?" I asked.

Dr. Biv shook his head no.

Scorecard:

Red Team: 0   Blue Team: 0   Green Team: 1

Dr. Biv took the flashlight from Tim. He placed it on a bench, along with two more white-light flashlights.

Then he blew his whistle. "Quick now! One person from each team! Run for a flashlight, and shine it on something that's your team color." He blew his whistle again for us to go.

My baseball cap! I could use that!

I took off, along with Carlos from the blue team and Phoebe from the green team. We reached the bench at the same time. I switched on the light, pointing it at my head.

But where was my red cap? It was gone. This race had nothing to do with science or quick thinking and I was still going to lose.

In a flash, Carlos shone his light on his jeans.

"Blue team is the winner!" announced Dr. Biv.

"Here's your cap," Arnold said, bringing it over to me. "You were in such a hurry, Ralphie, you didn't realize it fell off while you were running."

Scorecard:
Red Team: 0   Blue Team: 1   Green Team: 1

"How unlucky can you get?" I muttered. "It's not like Carlos's pants are going to fall off."

Carlos laughed. "Don't kid yourself, Ralphie. It's not luck, it's speed," Carlos bragged. "I'm so fast, I bet I can go faster than the speed of light."

The Friz clapped her hands. "Brilliant idea, Carlos! You can race your flashlight."

"Race my flashlight?" Carlos repeated.

"Certainly! Phoebe," the Friz said, "you can be our target, please." Ms. Frizzle directed

Carlos to stand next to Phoebe. Then she sent me to the other end of the gym.

"When I say go, Ralphie, you shine the flashlight on Phoebe. And you, Carlos, reach out and touch Phoebe's shoulder. We'll see who or what will reach Phoebe first, Carlos or the light."

I had to show Carlos he wasn't super-speedy. I couldn't mess up.

"Ready . . ." said Dr. Biv. "Set . . . Go!"

I flicked on the light. Instantly, a white circle lit Phoebe's shirt. Carlos reached out but he was too late.

Why Carlos Lost
by Wanda

Light travels approximately 186,000 miles per second (299,300 km/sec). Light moves faster than anything, even sound. That's why you see lightning before you hear thunder.

"Sorry, Carlos," the Friz said. "Nothing moves faster than light."

"Since Carlos lost, does the red team get a point?" I asked.

Dr. Biv shook his head. "The flashlight won, not the red team, Ralphie. The speed of light is a law of light. No points."

Scorecard:
Red Team: 0   Blue Team: 1   Green Team: 1
                Flashlight: 1

"Okay," Carlos grumbled, "so I lost to a flashlight. What other Color Day races are we going to do in the gym?"

The Friz laughed. "Color Day? In this dark gym? Lighten up, Carlos. We're going to the sun!"

CHAPTER 3

Everyone raced to the Magic School Bus. "This way, red team," I called, leading D.A. and Arnold to the back of the bus. No one would bother us there. We could discuss our strategy to win.

The blue team sat together in the front. Green was in the middle. Ms. Frizzle took her place behind the wheel.

Dr. Biv sat right behind the Friz. He bent his head, polishing his already shiny whistle.

"Get ready for blastoff!" Ms. Frizzle cried happily. She set a dial on the dashboard. The Magic School Bus reared up on its back wheels. It pointed straight to the sky like a rocket ship.

The Friz snapped her fingers and suddenly we were all wearing space suits in our team colors. Liz had a green mini-suit and even the Friz and Dr. Biv wore rainbow-colored ones.

Ms. Frizzle turned the ignition key. A fire ignited under the bus. "Ready for launch?" Ms. Frizzle yelled.

"Red team ready," I shouted over the roar of the Magic School Rocket.

"Speak for yourself," Arnold said under his breath.

"Green ready," Tim called out.

"Blue, too," Keesha added.

The Magic School Rocket rumbled and shook. Liftoff! We rose from the ground, farther and farther from the school, up, up, through clouds and sky.

"Uh, Ms. Frizzle? How far away is the sun?" Arnold asked.

"Quite a way," Ms. Frizzle answered. "About 93 million miles."

I whistled. "Well, if we want to get back to school for lunch, we'll have to move pretty quickly."

"Faster than the speed of light?" Carlos said with a wink.

What Is a Light-year?

by D.A.

A light-year is the distance light travels in one year: almost 6 trillion miles.

It may seem strange to use light as a measurement. But space is so vast that it would be hard to measure it in miles. So scientists who study space use light-years.

The star closest to Earth, other than the sun, is 4.3 light-years away. The distance from one end of our galaxy to the other is about 100,000 light-years.

Ms. Frizzle shook her head. "Remember, nothing moves faster than the speed of light, class. But if we were able to travel at light speed, it would take only eight minutes to reach the sun."

Eight minutes to get to the sun? Why couldn't I move like that? Then I'd never be late again! Even though we weren't going that fast now, we still zipped along.

We shot past the moon.

"It's so bright," said Phoebe. "Is the moon a source of natural light, too?"

"The moon doesn't have its own light," Dr. Biv said, turning around to speak. "It only reflects the light of the sun."

"White light!" said Wanda. "And it seems so bright because space is black."

Why Space Is Black
by Wanda

In space, there is no air or gas. There is nothing in space to absorb or reflect light. So light in space travels in straight lines with nothing to disturb it, and space always looks dark and black.

"Mercury up ahead!" the Friz announced. "The closest planet to the sun."

By the time I checked out the view, we'd left Mercury behind.

The Friz pulled a lever by the steering wheel. "Sun shield on!" she announced. "Super goggles on! These will protect your eyes from the brightness — and allow you to see each ray of light coming from the sun."

I peered through the sunglasses that somehow wound up on my nose. The sun was bright white and growing larger by the second. I couldn't even see the whole thing. We were getting so close! And it looked so different from the way it does on Earth. It looked like a giant ball of fire.

"How come the sun looks white?" Wanda asked. "It always seemed yellow when I looked at it before."

"That's because you were seeing it through Earth's atmosphere, which affects the color," the Friz explained. "Here in space you can see that the sun shines pure white light."

While the other teams oohed and ahed at the sun, I geared up for the next challenge. The red team hadn't won anything yet. I had to make sure we would win this one.

"Think, think, think, Ralphie," I told myself.

I glanced at Dr. Biv. He was sitting back

The Sun
by Carlos

Our sun is an average star, just like the billions of other stars in our galaxy. So why does the sun look so big? The answer is distance. Other stars are light-years away. Our sun is only light-minutes away.

The sun and other stars are not solid. They are collections of gases held together by gravity.

in his seat, relaxing. He pulled out a smooth round object from his pocket and began to polish it.

Well, maybe the next contest won't happen for a while, I decided. But I wanted to be ready. I wanted to win.

"Attention, please. We are now entering the sun's atmosphere, also known as the corona," the Friz announced. Out the window, things were changing. First we passed through these silvery streamers that looked kind of gauzy. Strange!

Next we passed through gases that had a reddish color. "This is the chromosphere," the Friz told us.

Even the color red wasn't enough to get my total attention. Not when I had a race to win.

The Magic School Rocket kept moving. Now, all around us, gases bubbled and churned. It reminded me of a pot of boiling water on the stove, just before I helped my dad put in the spaghetti to cook.

"We are in the photosphere," the Friz explained. "This is what we see from Earth. The photosphere is what we would call the surface, if the sun were solid."

I glanced at my team. D.A. flipped through pages of her book. Arnold fanned himself, as if he could really feel the heat from the sun.

"Get your head out of those books!" I hissed to D.A. "And Arnold, the temperature in here is the same as always. That's what the sun shield is for! Come on, we have to get in race-winning shape."

I raised my arms above my head. "Let's stretch. We need to be ready to move!"

"We already are moving," Arnold pointed out, "in a spacecraft."

He fanned himself even harder.

"D.A., Arnold!" I said. "We have to prepare. Everyone! Check your shoelaces!" I bent to retie my shoe.

Tweet! Dr. Biv's whistle sounded.

I popped back up.

"It's time for the next contest," Dr. Biv announced, "which I call Leap to Beep. This is a question-and-answer race. I will call out the questions. When your team knows the answer, send one member to the front of the bus." He held up the round object he'd been polishing. Different colored stripes covered every inch.

"What is that thing?" asked Keesha.

Dr. Biv placed the object on the dashboard, then pressed it. *Bzzzzz!* "It's my Rainbow Answer Buzzer," he said. "Whoever presses this first and has the correct answer wins!"

"Before you start," Ms. Frizzle interrupted, "look out the windows. We are now in the sun's core."

We looked around. The Magic School Rocket was smack in the middle of a wild raging fire.

"Wow," Phoebe said. "We never flew through fires like this at my old school."

From the Desk of Ms. Frizzle

At the center of the sun, the pressure and heat are so strong, gases crash together and create different gases. In the process, they release tremendous amounts of energy. The sun's core has a temperature of over 28 million degrees Fahrenheit (15.6 million °C).

"This isn't the kind of burning you see when you light a match or build a fire on Earth," the Friz told us. "What you're seeing is all the energy being released by the gases crashing together in the sun's center. Just a tiny amount of gas creates a huge supply of light and energy."

I had my own energy. A nervous kind of energy. I tapped my feet. I shook my shoulders.

I waited anxiously for Dr. Biv's first question of the race. I was glad now that D.A. was on my team — and glad, too, she'd been studying. Maybe she would know all the answers.

"Pssst!" I whispered to D.A. "If you know the answer, tell me. I'll run up to press the buzzer."

After all, I'd been stretching while D.A. and Arnold were just sitting. I'd be fastest.

"Good." Arnold nodded. "I'll just sit right here where it's safe."

Dr. Biv blew his whistle. "Listen up. First question: Which gases make up the sun?"

"I just read that!" D.A. wheeled closer to me. "It's hydrogen and helium. Go!"

I took off. Then I fell down. My shoelaces! I never finished tying them!

Phoebe raced up to press the buzzer while I struggled to stand.

"Hydrogen and helium," she announced. "I learned that at my old school."

Scorecard:
Red Team: 0   Blue Team: 1   Green Team: 2

The Sun's a Gas . . . or Two
by Carlos

The sun's gases are mostly
1) Hydrogen: an element that's also found in water
2) Helium: the element that makes balloons float in air

"Excellent!" said the Friz as I tied each of my laces with a double knot. "By the way,

we are now traveling away from the sun's core, along the same route that energy takes."

The Magic School Rocket sped along. "Thank you, Ms. Frizzle," said Dr. Biv. "The next question, coincidentally, is about this energy."

I sat forward, ready to run.

"As Ms. Frizzle mentioned, energy travels out from the core," said Dr. Biv. "It moves in small bundles, too tiny for us to see each one. Are these bundles of energy that make up light called neutrons, photons, or batons?"

D.A. elbowed me. "Photons!"

I scrambled for the front of the bus. Why, oh why, had I chosen a seat in the back? Keesha beat me to the buzzer.

"Yes, Keesha?" said Dr. Biv.

"Is it . . ." She hesitated. "Photons?"

"Correct!" Dr. Biv gave his whistle a sharp tweet.

Scorecard:
Red Team: 0   Blue Team: 2   Green Team: 2

"And now for the last question," Dr. Biv said. "How old is the sun: a) 4 to 5 minutes b) 100,000 to 200,000 years or c) 4.6 billion years?"

I jumped out of my seat. But Arnold jumped even faster. "I'd better get this one, Ralphie. Give yourself a break."

Before I could say a word, he took off.

Pretty fast, too, I'd have to admit. He beat Tim and Carlos to the buzzer.

"Four-point-six billion years!" Arnold exclaimed.

"You are right!" said Dr. Biv.

Scorecard:
Red Team: 1   Blue Team: Green Team: 2

All right! I high-fived D.A. and Arnold, too, when he came back. Our luck was changing. Now we were on a roll!

Dr. Biv put the buzzer back in his pocket. "That's it! Game over."

"Over?" I said. So much for being on a roll. Then I had an idea. "Hey, D.A.," I said. "Look in your books! If we find something Dr. Biv doesn't know about energy from the sun, maybe he'll give us bonus points!"

D.A. nodded.

First place, here we come!

CHAPTER 4

D.A. reached for a book. She scoured each page. Then she turned to me, excited. "I found something! All sorts of light come from the sun, including light we can't see."

"Really, D.A.?" I said loudly. I wanted Dr. Biv to hear every word. "You say there are uh, um . . . certain uh . . ."

"Kinds of light," Arnold put in helpfully.

"Right," I said. "Kinds of light we can see? And other kinds we can't?"

I glanced hopefully at Dr. Biv. He was listening. But was he impressed? Nope. He nodded, yawning. I guess that was old news for him. No bonus points for the red team.

But the Friz smiled at us. "Thank you for bringing that up, red team. That's something the other teams should know, too. Visible light and invisible light are both part of the electromagnetic spectrum."

"Um, Ms. Frizzle?" I said. "What exactly is the electric man spectacle?"

"That's the electromagnetic spectrum, Ralphie," D.A. corrected me. "According to my research, that's a term for all the different kinds of light waves found in a single ray."

What's in a Ray?
by D.A.

Energy travels away from the sun in waves. Each ray contains many different kinds of light, some of which our eyes can see and some of which are invisible. All this visible and invisible light makes up the electromagnetic spectrum.

"Waves?" I echoed. "Light travels in waves?"

D.A. nodded. "If you could see one kind of light traveling in a ray, like red light or green light, it would look sort of like zigzags or ripples. Each different kind of light has a different size wave."

Sized Up
by Keesha

Every kind of light has its own specific wavelength. A light's wavelength is the distance from the peak of one wave to the peak of the next. A light's wavelength is what determines whether or not we can see it.

Wanda raised her hand. "Ms. Frizzle, are light waves anything like ocean waves?"

"In a way," answered the Friz. "All waves — water waves, sound waves, light

waves — vibrate with energy. Light waves carry both electric and magnetic energy."

Ms. Frizzle pulled down a giant chart from the front of the Magic School Rocket. She waved at it grandly. "This, class, shows the entire electromagnetic spectrum, listed from longest wavelength to shortest."

Invisible light:

Gamma rays
X–rays
Ultraviolet rays

Visible light:

Red
Orange
Yellow
Green
Blue
Indigo
Violet

Invisible light:

Infrared rays
Microwaves
Radio waves

"Hey, red has the longest wavelength of all the kinds of visible light!" I said. "Is that good or bad?"

Ms. Frizzle laughed. "Wavelengths aren't the only differences among the kinds of light," she said. "Every light has a different energy level, too."

"How much energy does red have?" I asked.

Dr. Biv snapped up the chart. "Let's find out with a little race. I call this one Photon Finish."

"Uh-oh," said Arnold. "I think we're about to become photons."

The Friz winked. "Come on, Arnold, take a chance. Get energized!"

Before I could even blink, the Magic School Rocket shrank to a teeny-tiny size, and we all shrank with it. I looked down. I was wearing a supersleek black-as-space suit, almost like a scuba-diving outfit. We all were. And we were all shaking a little, too. Not with fear — with energy. At least, D.A., Arnold, and

I were shaking a little. The other teams seemed to be shaking a *lot*.

"Hey! This is so" — I stopped in midsentence to yawn — "exciting." Still vibrating, I sat down quietly in my seat. Arnold and D.A. sat next to me.

"Is it just me, or does everyone else seem to have a lot more energy than us?" I said.

D.A. sighed. "The longer the wavelength, the less the energy," she said. "Red's wavelength is longest, so . . ." She trailed off into a yawn.

I slumped in my seat. "No fair!" I said. "We have the least energy of all the teams. The red team doesn't stand a chance."

"How can we win a race?" Arnold spoke wearily. "We'll never travel as fast as the more energized teams!"

"Red is the worst color to be on Color Day!" I added.

Dr. Biv shrugged. "It's the law of light."

I wanted to protest, but I knew I'd better save my energy for the race.

"Ralphie, I know you're angry," the Friz said. "Or should I say, seeing red? But wait and see what happens. I bet you'll do better than you expect. On to the race!"

She guided the Magic School Rocket through the sun's atmosphere. All around us, sunbeams whizzed past.

How Wavelengths Measure Up
by Phoebe

Each wavelength of visible light is smaller than the thickness of one human hair. It would take 250 wavelengths of red light to equal the thickness of one sheet of paper.

"Everyone outside!" Ms. Frizzle crowed.

An escape hatch opened. One by one, we slipped through the opening, onto a platform.

"Nice sundeck," joked Carlos.

Of course, I was the last one out, with D.A. and Arnold just in front of me. We were hustling, but the other teams seemed much more energized!

"This is the first leg in a race back to school," Dr. Biv told us. "Each photon team will be part of a different sun ray. You'll travel in a wavelength that matches your team color."

"Just ride the waves . . . I mean wavelengths," Ms. Frizzle put in. "Dr. Biv and I will catch you at the finish line — the approximate place where Earth's atmosphere begins."

"Oh!" she said. "I almost forgot." The Friz snapped her fingers and suddenly we were all wearing headphones with little microphones attached. "Just a little device so we can all hear one another," Ms. Frizzle's voice came through the headsets.

"Cool!" said Wanda.

"You mean hot," Carlos said, pointing to the flaming sun. We all groaned.

"Ready, Ralphie?" D.A. nudged me.

"Sure," I said.

But I didn't think we stood a chance.

CHAPTER 5

I grabbed hands with D.A. and Arnold. The green team bunched together, and so did the blue. Thanks to our super sun goggles, we could see each single ray of light.

We all balanced, ready to jump at the same time.

"Ready, set, go!" Ms. Frizzle cried.

Before I could hesitate, D.A. jumped, pulling Arnold and me with her. We landed in the middle of a sun ray, and began zipping along, faster than I'd ever moved before. I couldn't see the other teams, but I didn't have a lot of time to look around. We were moving faster than anything. Riding the wavelength

was like being on a zigzaggy slide. The other colored wavelengths in our ray squiggled and vibrated all around us.

"How are we?" I called out. "Can you see the other teams?"

"I see Dr. Biv up ahead!" D.A. shouted. "I see the finish line!"

Dr. Biv held one end of a long rope. The rest of it floated out beside him. The finish line!

"Photons!" Dr. Biv's voice came through our headphones. "As you pass the finish line, grab hold of the rope."

We were almost there!

"Faster, faster," I shouted, but it was impossible to control our wavelength's speed. Still, it didn't look like the other teams had gotten there. We hadn't lost yet!

I reached out my hand as far as it could stretch and grabbed Dr. Biv's rope. So did Arnold and D.A. — and Carlos, Phoebe, Keesha, Tim, Wanda, and Liz. We had all reached the finish line at exactly the same time!

Dr. Biv blew his whistle and we all tumbled out of our wavelengths, into the Magic School Rocket.

"It was a tie!" Dr. Biv announced.

"A tie!" I shouted happily. "We didn't lose!"

"Well, we didn't exactly win, either," D.A. pointed out.

"But we had the least amount of energy," I reminded her. "Shouldn't we have come in last?"

"No, silly," Keesha said. "We were all traveling at the speed of light!"

Scorecard:
Red Team: 2   Blue Team: 3   Green Team: 3

"What fun is a race if you all always travel at the same speed?" Tim wanted to know.

"Yeah," agreed Keesha. "Why bother with the next leg?"

"Now that we're in Earth's atmosphere, this is a race of an entirely different color," Ms. Frizzle said.

The Object of the Game
by Carlos

Three things can happen when light hits an object
1) It may bounce off the object and reflect a color, as when a red wavelength hits a red brick.
2) It may pass right through, as it does through a clear window or water (this might slow it down or change its direction slightly).
3) It may be absorbed, giving up all its energy and disappearing, as when a ray of yellow light hits a red brick.

"What makes it so different?" Phoebe asked.

"When you raced through space, you all traveled on light rays going the same speed — the speed of light," the Friz said. "There was nothing in space to slow you down. But now your light rays will be passing through Earth's atmosphere. It's filled with tiny bits of gas and dust and other things that can change a light ray's course. You might be bounced around a bit," Ms. Frizzle warned, "or slowed down."

I glanced at Arnold. His expression said what I was thinking: uh-oh.

"Our next finish line will be just above the tallest building in town," the Friz said. "We don't want any of you photons hitting a solid object and being absorbed now, do we?"

Once again, we perched on the deck of the Magic School Rocket. Even though D.A., Arnold, and I still had less energy than the other teams, I felt hopeful. After all, we hadn't lost the last race. If the other teams got slowed down by the atmosphere, we might even win this one! Anything could happen.

The Friz began the countdown. "Ready, set — wait!" She stuck out her arm, holding us back. She took out some binoculars, aimed them toward Earth, and peered through.

"Just as I suspected," she said. "There's a cloud below. You'll never get through that."

"Let's wait it out," Arnold said quickly.

A few minutes later, the cloud had passed.

"Go, teams!" Ms. Frizzle said.

"Are you sure it's safe?" Arnold said. But I was already pulling him and D.A. onto a light ray. Before Arnold could gulp, we were racing through the atmosphere.

Right away I noticed we were moving slower than we had in space. And there was even worse news.

"Raindrop ahead!" I called.

"We're going to hit it!" Arnold cried.

Sure enough, we struck the big blob of water.

Now we were moving so slowly, I thought we might even stop.

"What's going on?" Keesha called into her microphone.

"You've all hit raindrops!" Dr. Biv's voice boomed through our headphones. "You're all part of a rainbow!"

I craned my neck to look down. I could see all the colors in a beautiful arc.

"You're absolutely right, Ralphie." Ms. [Friz]zle hurried down the aisle. "The next le[g of t]he race is straight to the ground. Firs[t tea]m to be reflected by something near the [sch]ool wins. Please remember, class, you nee[d to] choose a target that's your team color, s[o you]r light will be reflected, not absorbed. You [don]'t want to give up your energy and disap[pea]r!"

"Green team," Dr. Biv said. "What i[s you]r target, please?"

Tim, Phoebe, and Liz put their heads to[get]her. "That nice green leafy tree in front o[f sch]ool," said Phoebe. Liz nodded.

The blue team chose the big blue slide i[n the] school playground.

"Let's pick something big, too," Arnol[d wh]ispered, "so we won't miss."

"And something high," D.A. added, "so i[t wil]l be closer!"

"The whole school!" I shouted. "It's re[d bri]ck!" Everyone looked at me. "We choose th[e sch]ool," I said more quietly. "Right?"

"Right!" said D.A. and Arnold.

Ms. Frizzle buzzed by on the Magic School Rocket. "I've turned on my special Action-Freeze Machine. I thought you might want to stop moving, so you can really see what's happening."

"But what is happening?" I asked. "Where did the rainbow come from?"

A Trick of the Light
by D.A.

When a wave changes speed and direction, as a light wave does when it enters a raindrop, that's called refraction.

Glass, water, air, and clear plastic all refract light.

If you place a straw in a clear glass filled with water, you'll notice that the straw looks broken into two different pieces. This is an example of refraction.

"I think a raindrop works the same way as a prism," D.A. said. "White light passes through a raindrop and gets separated into all the different colors."

"Bingo!" the Friz said. "When a wave of light passes through a raindrop, it changes speed. In air, light travels very fast, but in water, the light slows down. This slowing down causes the light to bend. Each color wavelength travels at a slightly different speed and bends in a slightly different direction, creating a rainbow!"

"Hey," Tim said. "I just realized something. The colors in the rainbow are in the same order as they were when they came out in the prism."

"That makes sense," I said, "because the wavelengths are bent the same way. Hey! They're ordered from longest wavelength to shortest: red, orange, yellow, green, blue, indigo, violet."

"Yes, yes," Dr. Biv said a little impatiently.

"Doesn't anyone want to know who won the race?" he asked.

"The race is still on?" I said. " be called on account of rain? Just ball game?"

Ms. Frizzle grinned. "Now t been refracted by the raindrop, you make it to the finish line — remer wavelengths have all been bent ir directions."

Dr. Biv just said, "Red team farthest from the finish line. Blue closest to the finish line. Blue team v

Score Card:
Red Team: 2   Blue Team: 4   Green

"I know, I know," I muttered as blew his whistle and we all tumbled b the Magic School Rocket. "It's the law

Dr. Biv ignored me. He whippe cloth and began polishing his shoe sparkled almost like glitter.

"Excuse me," I said in a loude "Aren't we going to finish the race school?"

"Hey, that's not fair," said Wanda. "Won't the team with the closest target get there first?"

Ms. Frizzle shook her head. "Not necessarily — this race can be tricky. Remember, now that we're in our atmosphere, bits of dust, pollution, and gases can get in your way."

"Hit one of those," Tim told me, "and you'll go flying who knows where. And lose the race," he added with a grin.

If I still didn't feel so tired from being low-energy red, I would have had a comeback. But I didn't say a thing. I had to save all my oomph for the race.

"I'll point out a sun ray that's going the right way for each of your targets," Ms. Frizzle continued. "Then, everybody, go!"

CHAPTER 6

Once again, we could see each ray of light as it headed toward us. "I'm turning on the special Slo-Mo Machine," she told everyone, "to slow you down. I wouldn't want you photons to miss the fun just because you're so quick."

Then she gave me a gentle push. "That ray's aiming for the school building."

I moved forward a little. This was it! This was our chance to score! My heart pounded with excitement. "Relax now, Ralphie," I told myself. "Relax."

D.A. held one of Arnold's hands and one of mine. With my free hand, I reached up to give my cap a lucky pat. Oops! I knocked my baseball cap right off. I lunged for it.

"Go!" shouted the Friz.

Arnold and D.A. jumped. "Wait! My cap!" I called. I grabbed it, taking off a split second later. But it was a split second too long. I held everyone back, and —

"We're on the wrong sun ray!" Arnold cried.

"It — it — it will be all right," I stammered, hoping that was true. We were still heading toward the school. Our ray could still hit it.

I looked around for the other teams. There! To the left, I saw Wanda, Keesha, and Carlos, the blue team. They didn't seem very happy, either. They were bouncing as if they were jumping on trampolines. And they were going in the wrong direction. Not toward the blue slide in the playground, but back toward the sky, at a different angle.

"What's happening to the blue team?" Arnold cried.

Ms. Frizzle's voice came through our

headphones. "Wanda, Keesha, and Carlos are helping the sky look blue. I'm afraid they won't win this race. But they'll be fine. They're just being reflected in all different directions by gases in the air. It happens to a lot of blue light — that's what makes the sky look blue!"

Dr. Biv gave his whistle a sharp tweet and the blue team dropped back into the Magic School Rocket.

"Blue team deterred!" said Dr. Biv. "Due to a little process called Rayleigh Scattering, named after Lord John Rayleigh, the English scientist who discovered it way back in the 1870s."

Does this guy know everything about light? I wondered. But I was also pleased. For once, the law of light had worked in the red team's favor!

Behind me, I could feel Arnold squirming. We were fast approaching Earth. And who knew what would happen to us and our sun ray?

"Ms. Frizzle!" Arnold shouted. "Are we

going to make it to the school? Will we be re-flected? Will we be okay?"

"Arnold, Arnold, Arnold," said the Friz. "Don't think about what can go wrong. Think about what can go bright!"

We were neck and neck with the green team, which was riding a wavelength the next sunbeam over. They were doing a little bouncing themselves.

"Look!" said D.A. "We're pulling ahead."

"And look, Arnold!" I added. "We're right on target. The school is straight ahead."

Arnold gulped loudly. "Sure, but there's something in our way! Alert! Alert! Truck ahead!"

Oh, no! That meant trouble for the red team.

"When we hit that white truck, we'll be absorbed," D.A. said, her voice trembling. "Gone forever!"

CHAPTER 7

I tried swaying to the right, then the left. I was trying to steer our wavelength — trying to change direction so we wouldn't hit the truck. But I couldn't do a thing. We just kept speeding toward it. "Where's a speck of dust when you need one?" I shouted. "Hitting one would change our path."

"No dust here," Arnold said. "If there was, I'd be sneezing."

We were done for. Nothing could stop us.

"Maybe we'll hit a window," D.A. said hopefully. "Then our light ray could pass right through."

Ms. Frizzle buzzed by on the Magic School Rocket. "I've turned on my special Action-Freeze Machine. I thought you might want to stop moving, so you can really see what's happening."

"But what is happening?" I asked. "Where did the rainbow come from?"

A Trick of the Light
by D.A.

When a wave changes speed and direction, as a light wave does when it enters a raindrop, that's called refraction.

Glass, water, air, and clear plastic all refract light.

If you place a straw in a clear glass filled with water, you'll notice that the straw looks broken into two different pieces. This is an example of refraction.

"I think a raindrop works the same way as a prism," D.A. said. "White light passes through a raindrop and gets separated into all the different colors."

"Bingo!" the Friz said. "When a wave of light passes through a raindrop, it changes speed. In air, light travels very fast, but in water, the light slows down. This slowing down causes the light to bend. Each color wavelength travels at a slightly different speed and bends in a slightly different direction, creating a rainbow!"

"Hey," Tim said. "I just realized something. The colors in the rainbow are in the same order as they were when they came out in the prism."

"That makes sense," I said, "because the wavelengths are bent the same way. Hey! They're ordered from longest wavelength to shortest: red, orange, yellow, green, blue, indigo, violet."

"Yes, yes," Dr. Biv said a little impatiently.

"Doesn't anyone want to know who won the race?" he asked.

"The race is still on?" I said. "Shouldn't it be called on account of rain? Just like a base-ball game?"

Ms. Frizzle grinned. "Now that you've been refracted by the raindrop, you might not make it to the finish line — remember, your wavelengths have all been bent in different directions."

Dr. Biv just said, "Red team is on top, farthest from the finish line. Blue team is closest to the finish line. Blue team wins!"

Score Card:
Red Team: 2   Blue Team: 4   Green Team: 3

"I know, I know," I muttered as Dr. Biv blew his whistle and we all tumbled back into the Magic School Rocket. "It's the law of light."

Dr. Biv ignored me. He whipped out a cloth and began polishing his shoes. They sparkled almost like glitter.

"Excuse me," I said in a louder voice. "Aren't we going to finish the race back to school?"

"You're absolutely right, Ralphie." Ms. Frizzle hurried down the aisle. "The next leg of the race is straight to the ground. First team to be reflected by something near the school wins. Please remember, class, you need to choose a target that's your team color, so your light will be reflected, not absorbed. You don't want to give up your energy and disappear!"

"Green team," Dr. Biv said. "What is your target, please?"

Tim, Phoebe, and Liz put their heads together. "That nice green leafy tree in front of school," said Phoebe. Liz nodded.

The blue team chose the big blue slide in the school playground.

"Let's pick something big, too," Arnold whispered, "so we won't miss."

"And something high," D.A. added, "so it will be closer!"

"The whole school!" I shouted. "It's red brick!" Everyone looked at me. "We choose the school," I said more quietly. "Right?"

"Right!" said D.A. and Arnold.

"Hey, that's not fair," said Wanda. "Won't the team with the closest target get there first?"

Ms. Frizzle shook her head. "Not necessarily — this race can be tricky. Remember, now that we're in our atmosphere, bits of dust, pollution, and gases can get in your way."

"Hit one of those," Tim told me, "and you'll go flying who knows where. And lose the race," he added with a grin.

If I still didn't feel so tired from being low-energy red, I would have had a comeback. But I didn't say a thing. I had to save all my oomph for the race.

"I'll point out a sun ray that's going the right way for each of your targets," Ms. Frizzle continued. "Then, everybody, go!"

CHAPTER 6

Once again, we could see each ray of light as it headed toward us. "I'm turning on the special Slo-Mo Machine," she told everyone, "to slow you down. I wouldn't want you photons to miss the fun just because you're so quick."

Then she gave me a gentle push. "That ray's aiming for the school building."

I moved forward a little. This was it! This was our chance to score! My heart pounded with excitement. "Relax now, Ralphie," I told myself. "Relax."

D.A. held one of Arnold's hands and one of mine. With my free hand, I reached up to

give my cap a lucky pat. Oops! I knocked my baseball cap right off. I lunged for it.

"Go!" shouted the Friz.

Arnold and D.A. jumped. "Wait! My cap!" I called. I grabbed it, taking off a split second later. But it was a split second too long. I held everyone back, and —

"We're on the wrong sun ray!" Arnold cried.

"It — it — it will be all right," I stammered, hoping that was true. We were still heading toward the school. Our ray could still hit it.

I looked around for the other teams. There! To the left, I saw Wanda, Keesha, and Carlos, the blue team. They didn't seem very happy, either. They were bouncing as if they were jumping on trampolines. And they were going in the wrong direction. Not toward the blue slide in the playground, but back toward the sky, at a different angle.

"What's happening to the blue team?" Arnold cried.

Ms. Frizzle's voice came through our

headphones. "Wanda, Keesha, and Carlos are helping the sky look blue. I'm afraid they won't win this race. But they'll be fine. They're just being reflected in all different directions by gases in the air. It happens to a lot of blue light — that's what makes the sky look blue!"

Dr. Biv gave his whistle a sharp tweet and the blue team dropped back into the Magic School Rocket.

"Blue team deterred!" said Dr. Biv. "Due to a little process called Rayleigh Scattering, named after Lord John Rayleigh, the English scientist who discovered it way back in the 1870s."

Does this guy know everything about light? I wondered. But I was also pleased. For once, the law of light had worked in the red team's favor!

Behind me, I could feel Arnold squirming. We were fast approaching Earth. And who knew what would happen to us and our sun ray?

"Ms. Frizzle!" Arnold shouted. "Are we

going to make it to the school? Will we be re-flected? Will we be okay?"

"Arnold, Arnold, Arnold," said the Friz. "Don't think about what can go wrong. Think about what can go bright!"

We were neck and neck with the green team, which was riding a wavelength the next sunbeam over. They were doing a little bouncing themselves.

"Look!" said D.A. "We're pulling ahead."

"And look, Arnold!" I added. "We're right on target. The school is straight ahead."

Arnold gulped loudly. "Sure, but there's something in our way! Alert! Alert! Truck ahead!"

Oh, no! That meant trouble for the red team.

"When we hit that white truck, we'll be absorbed," D.A. said, her voice trembling. "Gone forever!"

CHAPTER 7

I tried swaying to the right, then the left. I was trying to steer our wavelength — trying to change direction so we wouldn't hit the truck. But I couldn't do a thing. We just kept speeding toward it. "Where's a speck of dust when you need one?" I shouted. "Hitting one would change our path."

"No dust here," Arnold said. "If there was, I'd be sneezing."

We were done for. Nothing could stop us.

"Maybe we'll hit a window," D.A. said hopefully. "Then our light ray could pass right through."

"I knew I should have stayed home to-day," Arnold moaned.

I squeezed my eyes shut just before we hit the truck's door . . . and bounced right off!

"Hey! We didn't get absorbed into nothingness!" Arnold said.

"I don't understand," D.A. said. "The truck isn't red, so why did we bounce off it?"

Suddenly, I understood. "We bounced because the truck is white . . . and white light is made from all the colors!"

"Very good, Ralphie," Ms. Frizzle said. "That's exactly right."

"We did it!" I shouted.

"Well, yes, you did it," Dr. Biv said. "But I'm afraid you did it in second place." He pointed out Tim, Phoebe, and Liz, who were already back on board the rocket.

"Green team was bounced a bit by the air. But they still hit their leafy target first."

Scorecard:
Red Team: 2   Blue Team: 4   Green Team: 4

No points for red. But for once, I didn't really care. We hadn't been absorbed into nothingness. We were here, we were red, and we could still win Color Day.

I was ready for anything.

CHAPTER 8

The Magic School Rocket landed, then popped back into a normal-sized school bus.

"Whew," said Arnold. "I'm glad I'm not a photon anymore!"

Tim raised his hand. "Ms. Frizzle? There's one thing about light and color that I still don't get," he said. "When we mixed all the colors of light together we got white light, right?"

"Right!" said the Friz.

"So how come when I mix together all the colors in my paint set, the paint turns kind of murky brown-black, not white?" Tim asked.

"Ah! Mixing paints and dyes and pigments is different from mixing light," said Ms. Frizzle. "Perhaps the next Color Day challenge will shed some light on how. This way!" She and Dr. Biv led us onto the school field. Three groups of paint cans were lined up on the grass.

Arnold grinned. "We're having Color Day in the school field now? Hooray! We can stay ourselves."

"That's right, Arnold," said Ms. Frizzle. "And it's time for relay races."

Dr. Biv polished his whistle for the fiftieth time that morning. "All right, teams," he said. He gave the whistle a sharp tweet.

"Now." Dr. Biv glanced at me. "Who can tell me the primary colors of paint?"

Was this a review? We had already learned about primary colors when we had the flashlight relays. Without a second thought, I raised my hand — first!

"Wait!" said D.A.

But Dr. Biv was already pointing at me. And besides, this was a no-brainer.

"Red, blue, green," I announced. I had a big grin.

"I'm sorry, Ralphie," the Friz said. "Those are the primary colors of light, not the primary colors for paint."

Tim wrinkled his forehead, thinking. "Primary colors are the colors you need to make all the colors, right? Well, I just got this new paint set that only has red, blue, and yellow paints. And it says it's all I need. So I guess it's red, blue, and yellow!"

Dr. Biv pointed to Tim. "Correct! One point for the green team."

Scorecard:
Red Team: 2   Blue Team: 4   Green Team: 5

Dr. Biv waved the teams onto the field. Each team had three open cans of paint — red, blue, and yellow — grouped in front of them.

Dr. Biv unrolled a huge white cloth on the other side of the field.

"The name of the game is Dump and Splash," said Ms. Frizzle. "Dr. Biv will shout

out a color. The team that mixes the paints to get the right one first wins. Oh, and one more thing," she added. "One person — or lizard — carries one can at a time."

Dr. Biv thought a moment. He blew his whistle. "Green!"

"Blue and yellow!" D.A. whispered to me. "I'll take the blue and dump it, then you follow with the yellow!"

"Got it!" I said as D.A. took off. I grabbed the yellow paint can and ran to catch up.

"You're in the lead!" Arnold shouted behind us.

I turned my head to look back at the other teams — and ran right into D.A.

"Oomph!" We collided. My paint can went flying. D.A.'s paint can went flying, too. Yellow and blue paint splattered all over me as the red and blue teams passed us.

I looked green.

I ran over to Dr. Biv. "Does this count? We made green!"

Dr. Biv shook his head and pointed at

the giant sheet already painted with the other
teams' green splotches.

"The color belongs there, Ralphie," Ms.
Frizzle said gently.

"Blue team wins!" Dr. Biv announced.

Scorecard:
Red Team: 2   Blue Team: 5   Green Team: 5

"Yellow and blue paint make green paint," said Ms. Frizzle. "Now let's mix those same colors of light."

Ms. Frizzle first held up a red light, then a green light and aimed them at the same spot on the sheet. The red and green light made yellow. Then Dr. Biv turned on a blue light. The blue light mixed with the yellow light made white light.

I trudged back to the starting line. My wet sneakers made squelching sounds on the ground. "Blue and yellow light make white light. Blue and yellow paint make green paint." I squelched up to D.A. and Arnold. "I'm sorry," I told them. "We lost because of me."

"That's okay, Ralphie," said Dorothy Ann. "You were just trying to win."

"At least you got a wild-looking outfit out of it," Arnold added, laughing.

I sat down. I blended nicely with the grass.

"I'm sitting the next one out, guys," I said. "I'm not doing our team any good."

Dr. Biv shone his whistle, then blew it

loudly. "For this next race, team members will race one at a time. Teams, are you ready?"

"Yes!" everyone but me shouted.

"Make black!"

"It's all three primary colors!" Keesha tried to whisper to her teammates. She was so excited, she was practically yelling. "Everybody, grab a can, and go one at a time."

"Wait!" said D.A. quietly to Arnold and me. "The sheet already has green on it."

"That's right!" said Arnold. "That's blue and yellow. So all we need to do is splash some red on it!"

"Go, Arnold!" said D.A.

Arnold took off, carefully balancing the red can of paint. Carlos was way ahead of him. Even Liz, holding the big can on her head, was beating Arnold. But our team only needed to make one trip.

When he reached the sheet, Arnold tipped the red paint onto a green spot.

Black!

Dr. Biv blew his whistle. "The red team wins!"

Scorecard:
Red Team: 3   Blue Team: 5   Green Team: 6

I jumped up to give Arnold and D.A. high fives. "Good going, guys," I said. Dorothy Ann had helped our team score. So had Arnold.

"But we're still losing." I shook my head, feeling bad. "And it's all my fault."

"It's not over until it's over, Ralphie," the Friz said cheerfully. "And there's more to come!"

CHAPTER 9

I wiped my paint-smeared hands on the grass, then stood up straight. The Friz was right — Color Day wasn't over yet. The red team could still make a comeback, and I was ready to help. "What's next?" I asked.

Dr. Biv polished the surface of his watch. "It's almost lunchtime," he told us.

Ms. Frizzle nodded and said, "Let's go inside."

Everyone headed into the classroom.

"Are we eating lunch, or having some sort of contest?" Wanda asked.

"Both," said Dr. Biv. "This is our final contest. Take out your lunches, please.

Whose lunch contains all the colors of the rainbow?"

"That would be seven colors!" Wanda exclaimed. "Who would pack so much food?"

Everyone looked at me. "Ralphie!" they cried.

I took out a bright red apple. An orange. Three slices of yellow cheese. Green spinach salad. A blueberry yogurt with a blue plastic spoon. And a jam sandwich that looked purple on the inside.

Red, orange, yellow, green, blue, purple . . . that was six colors. What was missing?

I pulled out a bunch of cookies coated in dark blue frosting.

"Is this indigo?" I asked.

"Yes, indigo!" declared Dr. Biv.

He held up my arm, like I was the champion of the day. I grinned. You had to hand it to good old Dr. Biv. He really came up with a great contest.

Scorecard:
Red Team: 4   Blue Team: 5   Green Team: 5

"Time to eat!" said the Friz.

Everyone dug into their lunch bags. Keesha pulled out a turkey sandwich. Carlos had some leftover spaghetti. Wanda's mom had packed celery sticks with peanut butter.

Dr. Biv walked around, examining everyone else's food.

He shook his head sadly. "All pretty dull."

Phoebe held up her sandwich. "Dull? This is delicious."

But I knew what Dr. Biv meant — I had noticed him polishing his whistle all day long. I held up my apple so it caught the sun rays filtering into the room. It was so shiny, it glowed.

"Extra bonus point for your apple, Ralphie," Dr. Biv said, admiring it.

I grinned at Dr. Biv. I just loved the guy!

Scorecard:
Red Team: 5   Blue Team: 5   Green Team: 5

I couldn't stop smiling at Dr. Biv. Then I noticed his uniform. I mean really noticed it.

It had stripes in all seven colors of the visible spectrum. And they were in the same order as the colors in a rainbow. Each stripe of color had a small letter printed on it. R for red, O for orange, Y for yellow, G for green, B for blue, I for indigo, and V for violet. Suddenly, I realized something about Dr. Biv.

"Your middle initial is G, right?" I asked.

Dr. Biv nodded.

"Roy G. Biv!" I shouted. "Your name is the visible spectrum! White light!"

"Very good, Ralphie," he said.

Well, I guess Dr. Biv had every right to be a know-it-all about light.

Dr. Biv winked at me. "And since Color Day is over, it is time for me to go." He stepped into the hall. There was a sudden flash of light. We ran to the door, but he was gone.

"Hey, what happened to Dr. Biv?" asked Keesha.

Ms. Frizzle smiled. "Let's just say it was time for him to light up another room."

"But who won Color Day?" I asked.

"We don't need Dr. Biv to figure that

out," Carlos said. He quickly scanned the scorecard. "Hey, it's a tie."

Scorecard:
Red Team: 5   Blue Team: 5   Green Team: 5

A tie? Just when the red team was making a comeback? All of a sudden, I didn't want the contest to end. I was having too much fun. And I was finally helping my team. The red team could still take first place. I knew it. We had to have one last race. And I knew a contest I could definitely win.

I picked up my sandwich and shouted, "First one to finish lunch is the Color Day winner!"

Join my class on all of our Magic School Bus adventures!

The Magic School Bus®

science CHAPTER BOOKS

op on the Magic School Bus for out-of-this-world adventure!

BDA 0-439-10798-9	MSB Chapter Book #1: The Truth about Bats	$4.99 US
BDA 0-439-10799-7	MSB Chapter Book #2: The Search for the Missing Bones	$4.99 US
BDA 0-439-10990-6	MSB Chapter Book #3: Wild Whale Watch	$4.99 US
BDA 0-439-11493-4	MSB Chapter Book #4: Space Explorers	$4.99 US
BDA 0-439-20419-4	MSB Chapter Book #5: Twister Trouble	$4.99 US
BDA 0-439-20420-8	MSB Chapter Book #6: The Giant Germ	$4.99 US
BDA 0-439-20421-6	MSB Chapter Book #7: The Great Shark Escape	$4.99 US
BDA 0-439-20422-4	MSB Chapter Book #8: Penguin Puzzle	$4.99 US
BDA 0-439-20423-2	MSB Chapter Book #9: Dinosaur Detectives	$4.99 US
BDA 0-439-20424-0	MSB Chapter Book #10: Expedition Down Under	$4.99 US
BDA 0-439-31431-3	MSB Chapter Book #11: Insect Invaders	$4.99 US
BDA 0-439-31432-1	MSB Chapter Book #12: Amazing Magnetism	$4.99 US
BDA 0-439-31433-X	MSB Chapter Book #13: Polar Bear Patrol	$4.99 US
BDA 0-439-31434-8	MSB Chapter Book #14: Electric Storm	$4.99 US
BDA 0-439-42935-8	MSB Chapter Book #15: Voyage to the Volcano	$4.99 US
BDA 0-439-42936-6	MSB Chapter Book #16: Butterfly Battle	$4.99 US
BDA 0-439-56050-0	MSB Chapter Book #17: Food Chain Frenzy	$4.99 US
BDA 0-439-56052-7	MSB Chapter Book #18: The Fishy Field Trip	$4.99 US

At bookstores everywhere!

Scholastic Inc., P.O. Box 7502, Jefferson City, MO 65102

Please send me the books I have checked above. I am enclosing $_____ (please add $2.00 to cover shipping and handling). Send check or money order—no cash or C.O.D.s please.

Name_____Birth date_____

Address_____

City_____State/Zip_____

Please allow four to six weeks for delivery. Offer good in U.S.A. only. Sorry, mail orders are not available to residents of Canada. Prices subject to change.

■SCHOLASTIC

MSBBKLST0504